W9-CGU-786

WANDA AND THE FROGS

BARBARA AZORE • ILLUSTRATED BY **GEORGIA GRAHAM**

Tundra Books

Stow - Munroe Falls
Public Library

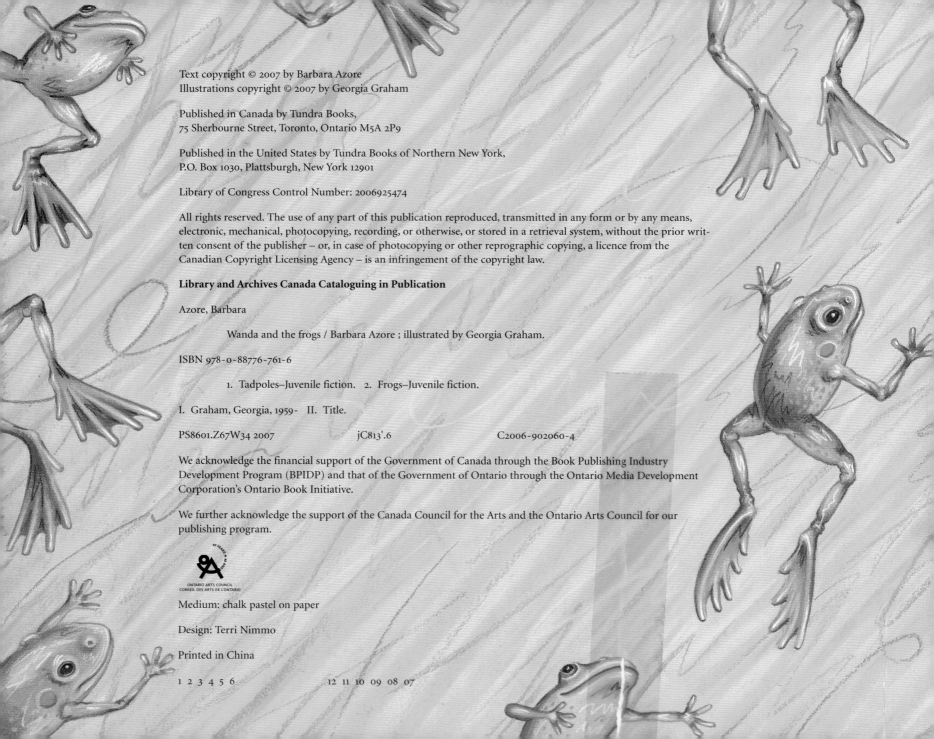

Text copyright © 2007 by Barbara Azore
Illustrations copyright © 2007 by Georgia Graham

Published in Canada by Tundra Books,
75 Sherbourne Street, Toronto, Ontario M5A 2P9

Published in the United States by Tundra Books of Northern New York,
P.O. Box 1030, Plattsburgh, New York 12901

Library of Congress Control Number: 2006925474

All rights reserved. The use of any part of this publication reproduced, transmitted in any form or by any means, electronic, mechanical, photocopying, recording, or otherwise, or stored in a retrieval system, without the prior written consent of the publisher – or, in case of photocopying or other reprographic copying, a licence from the Canadian Copyright Licensing Agency – is an infringement of the copyright law.

Library and Archives Canada Cataloguing in Publication

Azore, Barbara

    Wanda and the frogs / Barbara Azore ; illustrated by Georgia Graham.

ISBN 978-0-88776-761-6

    1. Tadpoles–Juvenile fiction.   2. Frogs–Juvenile fiction.

I. Graham, Georgia, 1959-   II. Title.

PS8601.Z67W34 2007   jC813'.6   C2006-902060-4

We acknowledge the financial support of the Government of Canada through the Book Publishing Industry Development Program (BPIDP) and that of the Government of Ontario through the Ontario Media Development Corporation's Ontario Book Initiative.

We further acknowledge the support of the Canada Council for the Arts and the Ontario Arts Council for our publishing program.

ONTARIO ARTS COUNCIL
CONSEIL DES ARTS DE L'ONTARIO

Medium: chalk pastel on paper

Design: Terri Nimmo

Printed in China

1 2 3 4 5 6   12 11 10 09 08 07

To Katherine, who loves every living creature
B.A.

To all the parents and children
who are curled up together for story time
G.G.

Something wonderful had happened. Wanda could feel it in the warm sun on her skin. She could hear it in the rushing creek and smell it in the May blossoms. Spring had come!

Walking home from school, Wanda came across a puddle beside the ravine. It had been left by the melting snow. Wriggling black tadpoles thrashed about in the shallow water.

The next morning, Wanda found her sand pail in the garage and, on the way to school, stopped at the puddle. It was smaller now. Wanda gently scooped some of the tadpoles into her pail. Very slowly, so that the water wouldn't spill, she walked to school.

The teacher was surprised when Wanda handed her
a pail of tadpoles. "Oh, my," she said, peering into the pail.
"Have you brought them for a visit? We'll have to find a
small aquarium to put them in."

The teacher went to the science storage room and found an aquarium just the right size. From the janitor's office, she borrowed an empty ice-cream bucket with a lid, then carried them back to the classroom. At recess, she took the ice-cream bucket to the creek and brought back some water, some pondweed, and two large rocks. Then she went to the pet store to buy some tadpole food.

Wanda gently poured the water and the tadpoles into the aquarium. The other children crowded round.

The teacher announced, "We will take care of the tadpoles until they become frogs."

For the next few days, the teacher taught the children about frogs. Everyone was excited and curious. Wanda felt proud when the teacher said, "It's a good thing that Wanda found these tadpoles. They would have died when the puddle dried up."

Wanda was made "tadpole monitor." She had to keep the children in order when they were standing around the aquarium and make sure the tadpoles were fed. Everyone had a chance to watch.

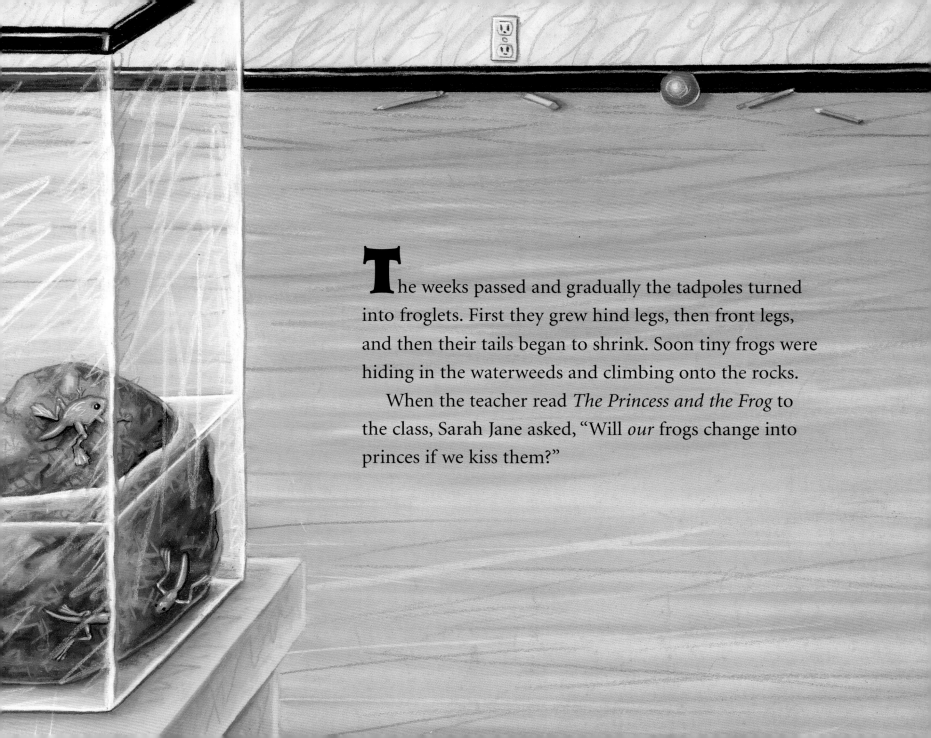

The weeks passed and gradually the tadpoles turned into froglets. First they grew hind legs, then front legs, and then their tails began to shrink. Soon tiny frogs were hiding in the waterweeds and climbing onto the rocks.

When the teacher read *The Princess and the Frog* to the class, Sarah Jane asked, "Will *our* frogs change into princes if we kiss them?"

One Friday morning, the teacher said to the children, "Before you go home today, say good-bye to the frogs. After school I am going to take them to the creek, where there are lots of bugs for them to eat."

All the children were sad. Wanda was miserable. She wanted to keep the frogs.

When the last bell rang, the children gathered round the aquarium and said their good-byes. Wanda waited until the very last child had left, and then she said to the teacher, "Miss?"

"Yes, Wanda?"

"Can I take some of my frogs home?"

"Oh, I don't know, Wanda. Will your mother let you keep frogs at home? You would have to feed them more now."

"I will!" said Wanda, thinking of all the flies and spiders that her mother hated having in the house. The frogs would eat them for her.

"Well, I suppose you did find them in the first place. Okay. I'll put a rock and some water and frogs in the ice-cream bucket."

Wanda slowly carried the frogs home and took them straight upstairs to her room. After supper, she removed the lid from the bucket, so the frogs could see and breathe.

During the night, one of the frogs discovered that he could climb the rock and leap over the top of the bucket. The other frogs soon followed. Across the bedroom floor they went, out through the door, along the hallway, and *plip-plop* down the stairs.

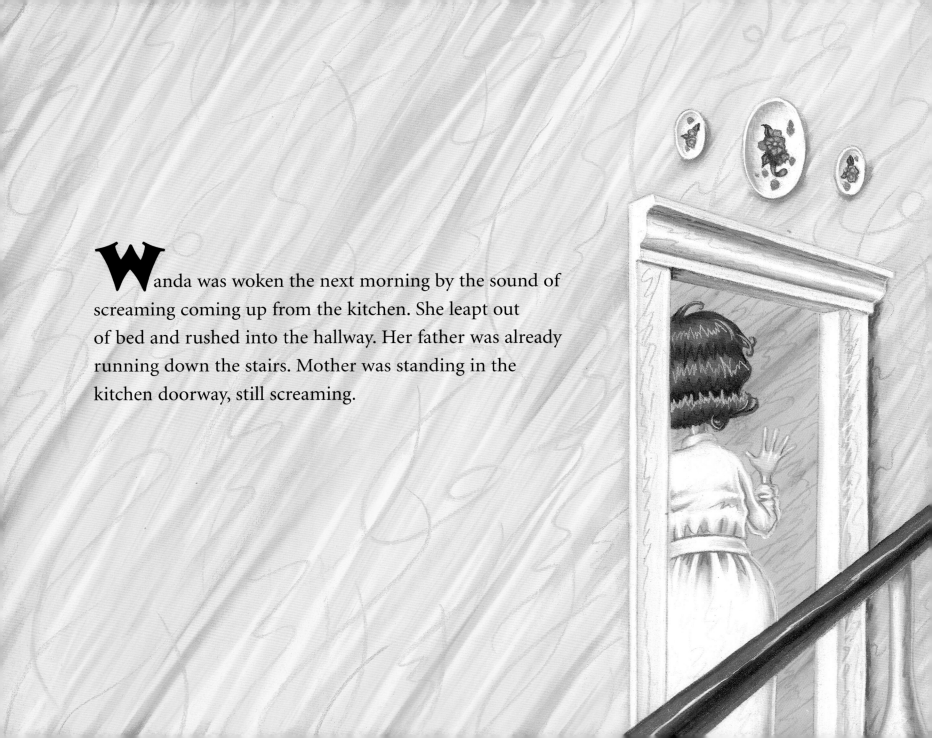

Wanda was woken the next morning by the sound of screaming coming up from the kitchen. She leapt out of bed and rushed into the hallway. Her father was already running down the stairs. Mother was standing in the kitchen doorway, still screaming.

"**T**here's a frog in the sink!" she shrieked. Daddy and Wanda peered in. "So there is," said Daddy.

Just then a second frog appeared on the kitchen table and a third popped out from behind the coffeepot. Soon there were frogs leaping all around the kitchen.

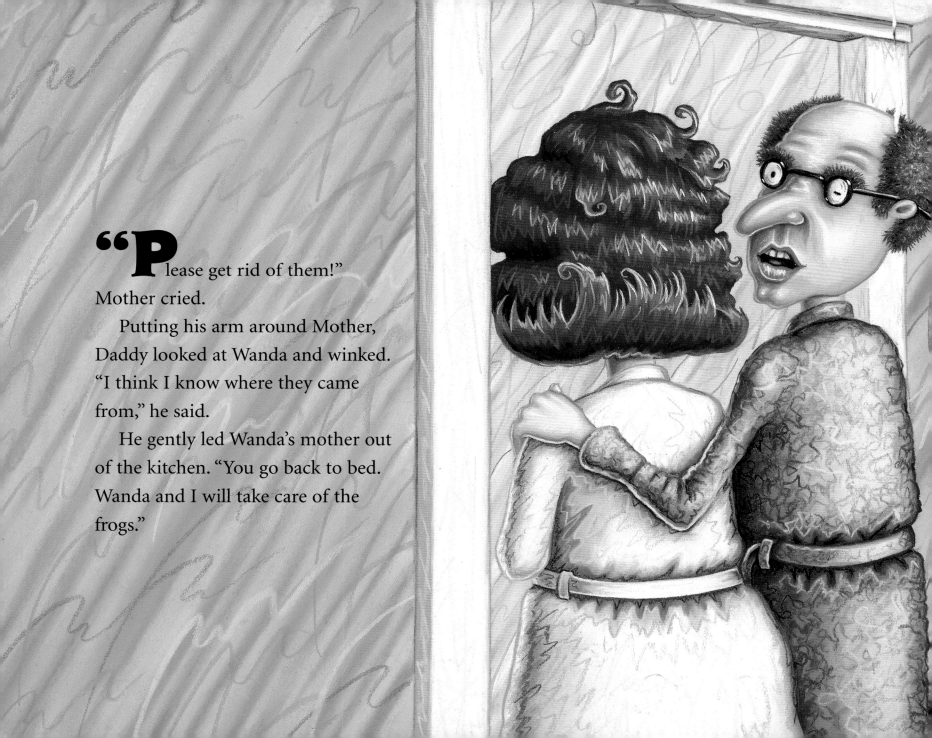

"Please get rid of them!" Mother cried.

Putting his arm around Mother, Daddy looked at Wanda and winked. "I think I know where they came from," he said.

He gently led Wanda's mother out of the kitchen. "You go back to bed. Wanda and I will take care of the frogs."

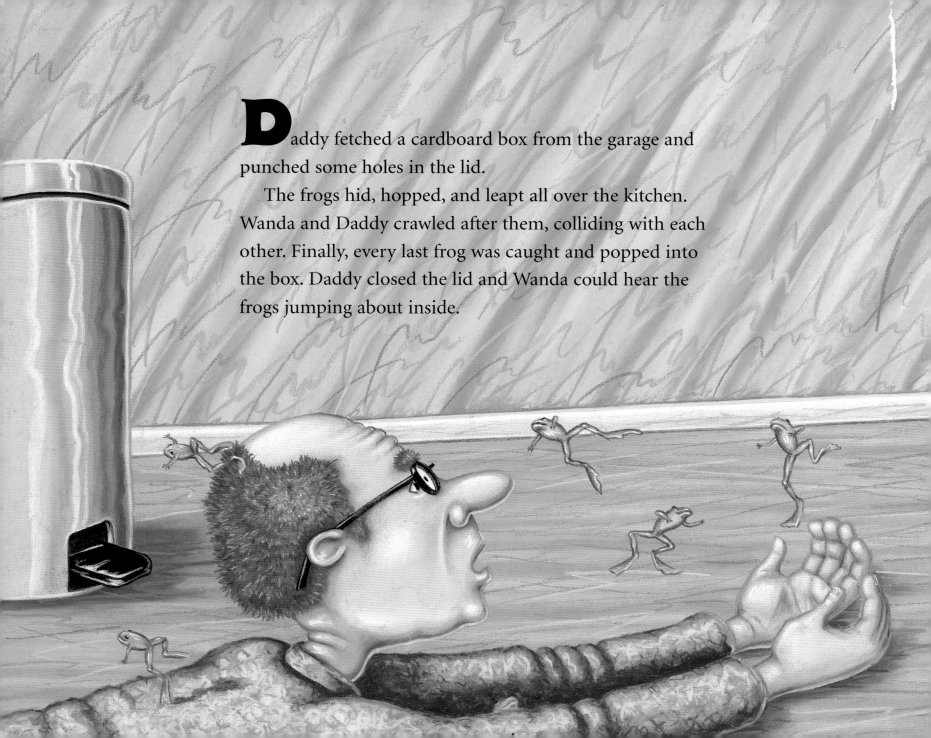

Daddy fetched a cardboard box from the garage and punched some holes in the lid.

The frogs hid, hopped, and leapt all over the kitchen. Wanda and Daddy crawled after them, colliding with each other. Finally, every last frog was caught and popped into the box. Daddy closed the lid and Wanda could hear the frogs jumping about inside.

"**N**ow, Wanda," he said, taking her by the hand. "Let's get dressed and take the frogs back to the creek, where they belong. Frogs don't like living in houses. They'll be much happier at the creek."

"Okay," said Wanda. "But I'll be able to visit them, won't I?"

"Yes, of course," said Daddy. "Perhaps this summer we can build a pond in the garden. One of your frogs might like to come and visit."